THE GREAT
SLAVE

BY

ZANE GREY

British Library Cataloguing-in-Publication Data
A catalogue record for this book is available from
the British Library

Contents

ZANE GREY

Pearl Zane Gray was born in Zanesville, Ohio (a town founded by his maternal ancestor Ebenezer Zane) in 1872. As well as being a keen reader of adventure stories and dime novels, Grey was a talented young baseball player, and won a scholarship to the University of Pennsylvania, from where he graduated with a degree in dentistry in 1898. Shortly before turning thirty, Grey moved to New York to set up his first dental clinic. He often left the city to go fishing and camping, and it was in 1900, while canoeing in the upper Delaware River, that he met Dolly, his future wife. The couple married in 1905, and when Dolly inherited a large sum of money, Grey was able to cease his dental practice and turn full-time to his nascent literary pursuits.

Dolly managed her husband's finances and contract negotiations – and tolerated his many infidelities – while Grey wrote, and the two of them split his income down the middle. His first magazine article, 'A Day on the Delaware', had been published in the May 1902 issue of *Recreation* magazine, but Grey found himself increasingly turning to Western fiction, having read Owen Wister's novel *The Virginian*. He struggled at first, even self-publishing his first work, *Betty Zane*. He followed this with its more successful sequel, *Spirit of the Border* (1906), his Grand Canyon inspired novel *The Last of the Plainsmen* (1908), *The Last Trail* (1909) and his first bonafide best-seller, *The Heritage of the Desert* (1910). But real success came in 1912, with *Riders of the Purple Sage,* Grey's best-known and most acclaimed novel, and one of the most popular works of Western fiction of all time.

Due to the financial success of *Riders of the Purple Sage,* Grey had the time and money to engage in his first and greatest passion: fishing. From 1918 until 1932, he was a regular contributor to *Outdoor Life* magazine, and as one of its celebrity writers did much to popularize big-game fishing. He continued to write prolifically in short bursts of inspiration for the rest of his life, and remained hugely popular; indeed, he became one of the first millionaire authors, and his total book sales now exceed 40 million. From 1925 to his death, he travelled a number of unspoiled lands, particularly the islands of South Pacific, New Zealand and Australia. Grey died in his home in Altadena, California, in 1939. Since his death, 110 films have been made that are based on his work.

The Great Slave

A voice on the wind whispered to Siena the prophecy of his birth. "A chief is born to save the vanishing tribe of Crows! A hunter to his starving people!" While he listened, at his feet swept swift waters, the rushing, green-white, thundering Athabasca, spirit-forsaken river; and it rumbled his name and murmured his fate. "Siena! Siena! His bride will rise from a wind kiss on the flowers in the moonlight! A new land calls to the last of the Crows! Northward where the wild goose ends its flight Siena will father a great people!"

So Siena, a hunter of the leafy trails, dreamed his dreams; and at sixteen he was the hope of the remnant of a once powerful tribe, a stripling chief, beautiful as a bronzed autumn god, silent, proud, forever listening to voices on the wind.

To Siena the lore of the woodland came as flight comes to the strong-winged wildfowl. The secrets of the forests were his, and of the rocks and rivers.

He knew how to find the nests of the plover, to call the loon, to net the heron and spear the fish. He understood the language of the whispering pines. Where the deer came down to drink and the caribou browsed on moss and the white rabbit nibbled in the grass and the bear dug in the logs for grubs – all these he learned; and also when the black flies drove the moose into the water and when the honk of the geese meant the approach of the north wind.

He lived in the woods, with his bow, his net and his spear. The trees were his brothers. The loon laughed for his happiness, the wolf mourned for his sadness. The bold crag above the river, Old Stoneface, heard his step when he climbed there in the twilight. He communed with the stern god of his ancestors and watched the flashing Northern Lights and listened.

From all four corners came his spirit guides with steps of destiny on his trail. On all the four winds breathed voices whispering of his future; loudest of all called the Athabasca, god-forsaken river, murmuring of the bride born of a wind kiss on the flowers in the moonlight.

It was autumn, with the flame of leaf fading, the haze rolling out of the hollows, the lull yielding to moan of coming wind. All the signs of a severe winter were in the hulls of the nuts, in the fur of the foxes, in the flight of waterfowl. Siena was spearing fish for winter store. None so keen of sight as Siena, so swift of arm; and as he was the hope, so he alone was the provider for the starving tribe. Siena stood to his knees in a brook where it flowed over its gravelly bed into the Athabasca. Poised high was his wooden spear. It glinted downward swift as a shaft of sunlight through the leaves. Then Siena lifted a quivering whitefish and tossed it upon the bank where his mother

Ema, with other women of the tribe, sun-dried the fish upon a rock.

Again and again, many times, flashed the spear. The young chief seldom missed his aim. Early frosts on the uplands had driven the fish down to deeper water, and as they came darting over the bright pebbles Siena called them by name.

The oldest squaw could not remember such a run of fish. Ema sang the praises of her son; the other women ceased the hunger chant of the tribe.

Suddenly a hoarse shout pealed out over the waters.

Ema fell in a fright; her companions ran away; Siena leaped upon the bank, clutching his spear. A boat in which were men with white faces drifted down toward him.

"Hal-loa!" again sounded the hoarse cry.

Ema cowered in the grass. Siena saw a waving of white hands; his knees knocked together and he felt himself about to flee. But Siena of the Crows, the saviour of a vanishing tribe, must not fly from visible foes.

"Palefaces," he whispered, trembling, yet stood his ground ready to fight for his mother. He remembered stories of an old Indian who had journeyed far to the south and had crossed the trails of the dreaded white men. There stirred in him vague memories of strange Indian runners telling campfire tales of white hunters with weapons of lightning and thunder.

"Naza! Naza!" Siena cast one fleeting glance to the north and a prayer to his god of gods. He believed his spirit would soon be wandering in the shades of the other Indian world.

As the boat beached on the sand Siena saw men lying with pale faces upward to the sky, and voices in an unknown tongue greeted him. The tone was friendly, and he lowered his threatening spear. Then a man came up to the bank, his hungry eyes on the pile of fish, and he began to speak haltingly in mingled Cree and Chippewayan language:

"Boy – we're white friends – starving – let us buy fish – trade for fish – we're starving and we have many moons to travel."

"Siena's tribe is poor," replied the lad. "Sometimes they starve too. But Siena will divide his fish and wants no trade."

His mother, seeing the white men intended no evil, came out of her fright and complained bitterly to Siena of his liberality. She spoke of the menacing winter, of the frozen streams, the snow-bound forest, the long night of hunger. Siena silenced her and waved the frightened braves and squaws back to their wigwams.

"Siena is young," he said simply; "but he is chief here. If we starve – we starve."

Whereupon he portioned out a half of the fish. The white men built a fire and sat around it feasting like famished wolves around a fallen stag. When they had appeased their hunger they packed the remaining fish in the boat, whistling and singing the while. Then the leader made offer to pay, which Siena refused, though the covetous light in his mother's eyes hurt him sorely.

"Chief," said the leader, "the white man understands; now he offers presents as one chief to another."

Thereupon he proffered bright beads and tinselled trinkets, yards of calico and strips of cloth. Siena accepted with a dignity in marked contrast to the way in which the greedy Ema pounced upon the glittering heap. Next the paleface presented a knife which, drawn from its scabbard, showed a blade that mirrored its brightness in Siena's eyes.

"Chief, your woman complains of a starving tribe," went on the white man. "Are there not many moose and reindeer?"

"Yes. But seldom can Siena creep within range of his arrow."

"A-ha! Siena will starve no more," replied the man, and from the boat he took a long iron tube with a wooden stock.

"What is that?" asked Siena.

"The wonderful shooting stick. Here, boy, watch! See the bark on the campfire. Watch!"

He raised the stick to his shoulder. Then followed a streak of flame, a puff of smoke, a booming report; and the bark of the campfire flew into bits.

The children dodged into the wigwams with loud cries, the women ran screaming, Ema dropped in the grass wailing that the end of the world had come, while Siena, unable to move hand or foot, breathed another prayer to Naza of the northland.

The white man laughed and, patting Siena's arm, he said: "No fear." Then he drew Siena away from the bank, and began to explain the meaning and use of the wonderful shooting stick. He reloaded it and fired again and yet again, until Siena understood and was all aflame at the possibilities of such a weapon.

Patiently the white man taught the Indian how to load it, sight and shoot, and how to clean it with ramrod and buckskin. Next he placed at Siena's feet a keg of powder, a bag of lead bullets and boxes full of caps. Then he bade Siena farewell, entered the boat with his men and drifted round a bend of the swift Athabasca.

Siena stood alone upon the bank, the wonderful shooting stick in his hands, and the wail of his frightened mother in his ears. He comforted her, telling her the white men were gone, that he was safe, and that the prophecy of his birth had at last begun its fulfilment. He carried the precious ammunition to a safe hiding place in a hollow log near his wigwam and then he plunged into the forest.

Siena bent his course toward the runways of the moose. He walked in a kind of dream, for he both feared and believed. Soon the glimmer of water, splashes and widening ripples, caused him to crawl stealthily through the ferns and grasses to the border of a pond. The familiar hum of flies told him of the location of his quarry. The moose had taken to the water, driven by the swarms of black flies, and were standing neck deep, lifting their muzzles to feed on the drooping poplar branches. Their wide-spreading antlers, tipped back into the water, made the ripples.

Trembling as never before, Siena sank behind a log. He was within fifty paces of the moose. How often in that very spot had he strung a feathered arrow and shot it vainly! But now he had the white man's weapon, charged with lightning and thunder. Just then the poplars parted above the shore, disclosing a bull in the act of stepping down. He tossed his antlered head at the cloud of humming flies, then stopped, lifting his nose to scent the wind.

"Naza!" whispered Siena in his swelling throat.

He rested the shooting stick on the log and tried to see over the brown barrel. But his eyes were dim. Again he whispered a prayer to Naza. His sight cleared, his shaking arms stilled, and with his soul waiting, hoping, doubting, he aimed and pulled the trigger.

Boom!

High the moose flung his ponderous head, to crash down upon his knees, to roll in the water and churn a bloody foam, and then lie still.

"Siena! Siena!"

Shrill the young chief's exultant yell pealed over the listening waters, piercing the still forest, to ring back in echo from Old Stoneface. It was Siena's triumphant call to his forefathers, watching him from the silence.

The herd of moose ploughed out of the pond and crashed into the woods, where, long after they had disappeared, their antlers could be heard cracking the saplings.

When Siena stood over the dead moose his doubts fled; he was indeed god-chosen. No longer chief of a starving tribe!

Reverently and with immutable promise he raised the shooting stick to the north, toward Naza who had remembered him; and on the south, where dwelt the enemies of his tribe, his dark glance brooded wild and proud and savage.

Eight times the shooting stick boomed out in the stillness and eight moose lay dead in the wet grasses. In the twilight Siena wended his way home and placed eight moose tongues before the whimpering squaws.

"Siena is no longer a boy," he said. "Siena is a hunter. Let his women go bring in the meat."

Then to the rejoicing and feasting and dancing of his tribe he turned a deaf ear, and in the night passed alone under the shadow of Old Stoneface, where he walked with the spirits of his ancestors and believed the voices on the wind.

Before the ice locked the ponds Siena killed a hundred moose and reindeer. Meat and fat and oil and robes changed the world for the Crow tribe.

Fires burned brightly all the long winter; the braves awoke from their stupor and chanted no more; the women sang of the Siena who had come, and prayed for summer wind and moonlight to bring his bride.

Spring went by, summer grew into blazing autumn, and Siena's fame and wonder of the shooting stick spread through the length and breadth of the land.

Another year passed, then another, and Siena was the great chief of the rejuvenated Crows. He had grown into a warrior's stature, his face had the beauty of the god-chosen, his eye the falcon flash of the Sienas of old. Long communion in the shadow of Old Stoneface had added wisdom to his other gifts; and now to his worshipping tribe all that was needed to complete the prophecy of his birth was the coming of an alien bride.

* * *

It was another autumn, with the wind whipping the tamaracks and moaning in the pines, and Siena stole along a brown, fern-lined trail. The dry smell of fallen leaves filled his nostrils; he tasted snow in the keen breezes. The flowers were dead, and still no dark-eyed bride sat in his wigwam. Siena sorrowed and strengthened his heart to wait. He saw her flitting in the shadows around him, a wraith with dusky eyes veiled by dusky wind-blown hair, and ever she hovered near him, whispering from every dark pine, from every waving tuft of grass.

To her whispers he replied: "Siena waits."

He wondered of what alien tribe she would come. He hoped not of the unfriendly Chippewayans or the far-distant Blackfeet; surely not of the hostile Crees, life enemies of his tribe, destroyers of its once puissant strength, jealous now of its resurging power.

Other shadows flitted through the forest, spirits that rose silently from the graves over which he trod, and warned him of double steps on his trail, of unseen foes watching him from the dark coverts. His braves had repeated gossip, filterings from stray Indian wanderers, hinting of plots against the risen Siena. To all these he gave no heed, for was not he Siena, god-chosen, and had he not the wonderful shooting stick?

It was the season that he loved, when dim forest and hazy fernland spoke most impellingly. The tamaracks talked to him, the poplars bowed as he passed, and the pines sang for him alone. The dying vines twined about his feet and clung to him, and the brown ferns, curling sadly, waved him a welcome that was a farewell. A bird twittered a plaintive note and a loon whistled a lonely call. Across the wide grey hollows and meadows of white moss moaned the north wind, bending all before it, blowing full into Siena's face with its bitter promise. The lichen-covered rocks and the rugged-barked trees and the creatures that moved among them – the whole world of earth and air heard Siena's step on the rustling leaves and a thousand voices hummed in the autumn stillness.

So he passed through the shadowy forest and over the grey muskeg flats to his hunting place. With his birch-bark horn he blew the call of the moose. He alone of hunting Indians had the perfect moose call. There, hidden within a thicket, he waited, calling and listening till an angry reply bellowed from the depths of a hollow, and a bull moose, snorting fight, came cracking the saplings in his rush. When he sprang fierce and bristling into the glade, Siena killed him. Then, laying his shooting stick over a log, he drew his knife and approached the beast.

A snapping of twigs alarmed Siena and he whirled upon the defensive, but too late to save himself. A band of Indians pounced upon him and bore him to the ground. One wrestling heave Siena made, then he was overpowered and bound. Looking upward, he knew his captors, though he had never seen them before; they were the lifelong foes of his people, the fighting Crees.

A sturdy chief, bronze of face and sinister of eye, looked grimly down upon his captive. "Baroma makes Siena a slave."

Siena and his tribe were dragged far southward to the land of the Crees. The young chief was bound upon a block in the centre of the village where hundreds of Crees spat upon him, beat him and outraged him in every way their cunning could devise. Siena's gaze was on the north and his face showed no sign that he felt the torments.

At last Baroma's old advisers stopped the spectacle, saying: "This is a man!"

Siena and his people became slaves of the Crees. In Baroma's lodge, hung upon caribou antlers, was the wonderful shooting stick with Siena's powder horn and bullet pouch, objects of intense curiosity and fear.

None knew the mystery of this lightning-flashing, thunder-dealing thing; none dared touch it.

The heart of Siena was broken; not for his shattered dreams or the end of his freedom, but for his people. His fame had been their undoing. Slaves to the murderers of his forefathers! His spirit darkened, his soul sickened; no more did sweet voices sing to him on the wind, and his mind dwelt apart from his body among shadows and dim shapes.

Because of his strength he was worked like a dog at hauling packs and carrying wood; because of his frame he was set to cleaning fish and washing vessels with the squaws. Seldom did he get to speak a word to his mother or any of his people. Always he was driven.

One day, when he lagged almost fainting, a maiden brought him water to drink. Siena looked up, and all about him suddenly brightened, as when sunlight bursts from cloud.

"Who is kind to Siena?" he asked, drinking.

"Baroma's daughter," replied the maiden.

"What is her name?"

Quickly the maiden bent her head, veiling dusky eyes with dusky hair. "Emihiyah."

"Siena has wandered on lonely trails and listened to voices not meant for other ears. He has heard the music of Emihiyah on the winds. Let the daughter of Siena's great foe not fear to tell of her name."

"Emihiyah means a wind kiss on the flowers in the moonlight," she whispered shyly and fled.

Love came to the last of the Sienas and it was like a glory. Death shuddered no more in Siena's soul. He saw into the future, and out of his gloom he rose again, god-chosen in his own sight, with such added beauty to his stern face and power to his piercing eye and strength to his lofty frame that the Crees quailed before him and marvelled. Once more sweet voices came to him, and ever on the soft winds were songs of the dewy moorlands to the northward, songs of the pines and the laugh of the loon and of the rushing, green-white, thundering Athabasca, god-forsaken river.

Siena's people saw him strong and patient, and they toiled on, unbroken, faithful. While he lived, the pride of Baroma was vaunting. "Siena waits" were the simple words he said to his mother, and she repeated them as wisdom. But the flame in his eye was like the leaping Northern Lights, and it kept alive the fire deep down in their breasts.

In the winter when the Crees lolled in their wigwams, when less labour fell to Siena, he set traps in the snow trails for silver fox and marten. No Cree had ever been such a trapper as Siena. In the long months he captured many furs, with which he wrought a robe the like of which had not before been the delight of a maiden's eye. He kept it by him for seven nights, and always during this time his ear was turned to the wind. The seventh night was the night of the midwinter feast, and when the torches burned bright in front of Baroma's lodge Siena took the robe and, passing slowly and stately till he stood before Emihiyah, he laid it at her feet.

Emihiyah's dusky face paled, her eyes that shone like stars drooped behind her flying hair, and all her slender body trembled.

"Slave!" cried Baroma, leaping erect. "Come closer that Baroma may see what kind of a dog approaches Emihiyah."

Siena met Baroma's gaze, but spoke no word. His gift spoke for him. The hated slave had dared to ask in marriage the hand of the proud Baroma's daughter. Siena towered in the firelight with something in his presence that for a moment awed beholders. Then the passionate and untried braves broke the silence with a clamour of the wolf pack.

Tillimanqua, wild son of Baroma, strung an arrow to his bow and shot into Siena's hip, where it stuck, with feathered shaft quivering.

The spring of the panther was not swifter than Siena; he tossed Tillimanqua into the air and, flinging him down, trod on his neck and wrenched the bow away. Siena pealed out the long-drawn war whoop of his tribe that had not been heard for a hundred years, and the terrible cry stiffened the Crees in their tracks.

Then he plucked the arrow from his hip and, fitting it to the string, pointed the gory flint head at Tillimanqua's eyes and began to bend the bow. He bent the tough wood till the ends almost met, a feat of exceeding great strength, and thus he stood with brawny arms knotted and stretched.

A scream rent the suspense. Emihiyah fell upon her knees. "Spare Emihiyah's brother!"

Siena cast one glance at the kneeling maiden, then, twanging the bowstring, he shot the arrow toward the sky.

"Baroma's slave is Siena," he said, with scorn like the lash of a whip. "Let the Cree learn wisdom."

Then Siena strode away, with a stream of dark blood down his thigh, and went to his brush tepee, where he closed his wound.

In the still watches of the night, when the stars blinked through the leaves and the dew fell, when Siena burned and throbbed in pain, a shadow passed between his weary eyes and the pale light. And a voice that was not one of the spirit voices on the wind called softly over him, "Siena! Emihiyah comes."

The maiden bound the hot thigh with a soothing balm and bathed his fevered brow.

Then her hands found his in tender touch, her dark face bent low to his, her hair lay upon his cheek. "Emihiyah keeps the robe," she said.

"Siena loves Emihiyah," he replied.

"Emihiyah loves Siena," she whispered.

She kissed him and stole away.

On the morrow Siena's wound was as if it had never been; no eye saw his pain. Siena returned to his work and his trapping. The winter melted into spring, spring flowered into summer, summer withered into autumn.

Once in the melancholy days Siena visited Baroma in his wigwam. "Baroma's hunters are slow. Siena sees a famine in the land."

"Let Baroma's slave keep his place among the squaws," was the reply.

That autumn the north wind came a moon before the Crees expected it; the reindeer took their annual march farther south; the moose herded warily in open groves; the whitefish did not run, and the seven-year pest depleted the rabbits.

When the first snow fell Baroma called a council and then sent his hunting braves far and wide.

One by one they straggled back to camp, footsore and hungry, and each with the same story. It was too late.

A few moose were in the forest, but they were wild and kept far out of range of the hunter's arrows, and there was no other game.

A blizzard clapped down upon the camp, and sleet and snow whitened the forest and filled the trails. Then winter froze everything in icy clutch. The old year drew to a close.

The Crees were on the brink of famine. All day and all night they kept up their chanting and incantations and beating of tom-toms to conjure the return of the reindeer. But no reindeer appeared.

It was then that the stubborn Baroma yielded to his advisers and consented to let Siena save them from starvation by means of his wonderful shooting stick.

Accordingly Baroma sent word to Siena to appear at his wigwam.

Siena did not go, and said to the medicine men: "Tell Baroma soon it will be for Siena to demand."

Then the Cree chieftain stormed and stamped in his wigwam and swore away the life of his slave. Yet again the wise medicine men prevailed. Siena and the wonderful shooting stick would be the salvation of the Crees. Baroma, muttering deep in his throat like distant thunder, gave sentence to starve Siena until he volunteered to go forth and hunt, or let him be the first to die.

The last scraps of meat, except a little hoarded in Baroma's lodge, were devoured, and then began the boiling of bones and skins to make a soup to sustain life. The cold days passed and a silent gloom pervaded the camp. Sometimes a cry of a bereaved mother, mourning for a starved child, wailed through the darkness. Siena's people, long used to starvation, did not suffer or grow weak so soon as the Crees. They were of hardier frame, and they were upheld by faith in their chief. When he would sicken it would be time for them to despair. But Siena walked erect as in the days of his freedom, nor did he stagger under the loads of firewood, and there was a light on his face. The Crees, knowing of Baroma's order that Siena should be the first to perish of starvation, gazed at the slave first in awe, then in fear. The last of the Sienas was succoured by the spirits.

But god-chosen though Siena deemed himself, he knew it was not by the spirits that he was fed in this time of famine. At night in the dead stillness, when even no mourning of wolf came over the frozen wilderness, Siena lay in his brush tepee close and warm under his blanket. The wind was faint and low, yet still it brought the old familiar voices. And it bore another sound – the soft fall of a moccasin on the snow. A shadow passed between Siena's eyes and the pale light.

"Emihiyah comes," whispered the shadow and knelt over him.

She tendered a slice of meat which she had stolen from Baroma's scanty hoard as he muttered and growled in uneasy slumber. Every night since her father's order to starve Siena, Emihiyah had made this perilous errand.

And now her hand sought his and her dusky hair swept his brow. "Emihiyah is faithful," she breathed low.

"Siena only waits," he replied.

She kissed him and stole away.

Cruel days fell upon the Crees, before Baroma's pride was broken. Many children died and some of the mothers were beyond help. Siena's people kept their strength, and he himself showed no effect of hunger. Long ago the Cree women had deemed him superhuman, that the Great Spirit fed him from the happy hunting grounds.

At last Baroma went to Siena. "Siena may save his people and the Crees."

Siena regarded him long, then replied: "Siena waits."

"Let Baroma know. What does Siena wait for? While he waits we die."

Siena smiled his slow, inscrutable smile and turned away.

Baroma sent for his daughter and ordered her to plead for her life.

Emihiyah came, fragile as a swaying reed, more beautiful than a rose choked in a tangled thicket, and she stood before Siena with doe eyes veiled. "Emihiyah begs Siena to save her and the tribe of Crees."

"Siena waits," replied the slave.

Baroma roared his fury and bade his braves lash the slave. But the blows fell from feeble arms and Siena laughed at his captors.

Then, like a wild lion unleashed from long thrall, he turned upon them: "Starve! Cree dogs! Starve! When the

Crees all fall like leaves in autumn, then Siena and his people will go back to the north."

Baroma's arrogance left him then, and on another day, when Emihiyah lay weak and palid in his wigwam and the pangs of hunger gnawed at his own vitals, he again sought Siena. "Let Siena tell for what he waits."

Siena rose to his lofty height and the leaping flame of the Northern Light gathered in his eyes. "Freedom!" One word he spoke and it rolled away on the wind.

"Baroma yields," replied the Cree, and hung his head.

"Send the squaws who can walk and the braves who can crawl out upon Siena's trail."

Then Siena went to Baroma's lodge and took up the wonderful shooting stick and, loading it, he set out upon snowshoes into the white forest. He knew where to find the moose yards in the sheltered corners. He heard the bulls pounding the hard-packed snow and cracking their antlers on the trees. The wary beasts would not have allowed him to steal close, as a warrior armed with a bow must have done, but Siena fired into the herd at long range. And when they dashed off, sending the snow up like a spray, a huge black bull lay dead. Siena followed them as they floundered through the drifts, and whenever he came within range he shot again. When five moose were killed he turned upon his trail to find almost the whole Cree tribe had followed him and were tearing the meat and crying out in a kind of crazy joy. That night the fires burned before the wigwams, the earthen pots steamed and there was great rejoicing. Siena hunted the next day, and the next, and for ten days he went into the white forest with his wonderful shooting stick, and eighty moose fell to his unerring aim.

The famine was broken and the Crees were saved.

When the mad dances ended and the feasts were over, Siena appeared before Baroma's lodge. "Siena will lead his people northward."

Baroma, starving, was a different chief from Baroma well fed and in no pain. All his cunning had returned. "Siena goes free. Baroma gave his word. But Siena's people remain slaves."

"Siena demanded freedom for himself and his people," said the younger chief.

"Baroma heard no word of Siena's tribe. He would not have granted freedom for them. Siena's freedom was enough."

"The Cree twists the truth. He knows Siena would not go without his people. Siena might have remembered Baroma's cunning. The Crees were ever liars."

Baroma stalked before his fire with haughty presence. About him in the circle of light sat his medicine men, his braves and squaws. "The Cree is kind. He gave his word. Siena is free. Let him take his wonderful shooting stick and go back to the north."

Siena laid the shooting stick at Baroma's feet and likewise the powder horn and bullet pouch. Then he folded his arms, and his falcon eyes looked far beyond Baroma to the land of the changing lights and the old home on the green-white, rushing Athabasca, god-forsaken river. "Siena stays."

Baroma started in amazement and anger. "Siena makes Baroma's word idle. Begone!"

"Siena stays!"

The look of Siena, the pealing reply, for a moment held the chief mute. Slowly Baroma stretched wide his arms and lifted them, while from his face flashed a sullen wonder. "Great Slave!" he thundered.

So was respect forced from the soul of the Cree, and the name thus wrung from his jealous heart was one to live for ever in the lives and legends of Siena's people.

Baroma sought the silence of his lodge, and his medicine men and braves dispersed, leaving Siena standing in the circle, a magnificent statue facing the steely north.

* * *

From that day insult was never offered to Siena, nor word spoken to him by the Crees, nor work given. He was free to come and go where he willed, and he spent his time in lessening the tasks of his people.

The trails of the forest were always open to him, as were the streets of the Cree village. If a brave met him, it was to step aside; if a squaw met him, it was to bow her head; if a chief met him, it was to face him as warriors faced warriors.

One twilight Emihiyah crossed his path, and suddenly she stood as once before, like a frail reed about to break in the wind. But Siena passed on. The days went by and each one brought less labour to Siena's people, until that one came wherein there was no task save what they set themselves. Siena's tribe were slaves, yet not slaves.

The winter wore by and the spring and the autumn, and again Siena's fame went abroad on the four winds. The Chippewayans journeyed from afar to see the Great Slave, and likewise the Blackfeet and the Yellow Knives. Honour would have been added to fame; councils called; overtures made to the sombre Baroma on behalf of the Great Slave, but Siena passed to and fro among his people, silent and cold to all others, true to the place which his great foe had given him. Captive to a lesser chief, they said; the Great Slave who would yet free his tribe and gather to him a new and powerful nation.

Once in the late autumn Siena sat brooding in the twilight by Ema's tepee. That night all who came near him were silent. Again Siena was listening to voices on the wind, voices that had been still for long, which he had tried to forget. It was the north wind, and it whipped the spruces and moaned through the pines. In its cold breath it bore a message to Siena, a hint of coming winter and a call from Naza, far north of the green-white, thundering Athabasca, river without a spirit.

In the darkness when the camp slumbered Siena faced the steely north. As he looked a golden shaft, arrow-shaped and arrow-swift, shot to the zenith.

"Naza!" he whispered to the winds. "Siena watches."

Then the gleaming, changing Northern Lights painted a picture of gold and silver bars, of flushes pink as shell, of opal fire and sunset red; and it was a picture of Siena's life from the moment the rushing Athabasca rumbled his name, to the far distant time when he would say farewell to his great nation and pass for ever to the retreat of the winds. God-chosen he was, and had power to read the story in the sky.

Seven nights Siena watched in the darkness; and on the seventh night, when the golden flare and silver shafts faded in the north, he passed from tepee to tepee, awakening his people. "When Siena's people hear the sound of the shooting stick let them cry greatly: Siena kills Baroma! Siena kills Baroma!"

With noiseless stride Siena went among the wigwams and along the lanes until he reached Baroma's lodge. Entering the dark he groped with his hands upward to a moose's antlers and found the shooting stick. Outside he fired it into the air.

Like a lightning bolt the report ripped asunder the silence, and the echoes clapped and reclapped from the cliffs. Sharp on the dying echoes Siena bellowed his war whoop, and it was the second time in a hundred years for foes to hear that terrible, long-drawn cry.

Then followed the shrill yells of Siena's people: "Siena kills Baroma . . . Siena kills Baroma . . . Siena kills Baroma!"

The slumber of the Crees awoke to a babel of many voices; it rose hoarsely on the night air, swelled hideously into a deafening roar that shook the earth.

In this din of confusion and terror when the Crees were lamenting the supposed death of Baroma and screaming in each other's ears, "The Great Slave takes his freedom!" Siena ran to his people and, pointing to the north, drove them before him.

Single file, like a long line of flitting spectres, they passed out of the fields into the forest. Siena kept close on their trail, ever looking backward, and ready with the shooting stick.

The roar of the stricken Crees softened in his ears and at last died away.

Under the black canopy of whispering leaves, over the grey, mist-shrouded muskeg flats, around the glimmering reed-bordered ponds, Siena drove his people.

All night Siena hurried them northward and with every stride his heart beat higher. Only he was troubled by a sound like a voice that came to him on the wind.

But the wind was now blowing in his face, and the sound appeared to be at his back. It followed on his trail as had the step of destiny. When he strained his ears he could not hear it, yet when he had gone on swiftly, persuaded it was only fancy, then the voice that was not a voice came haunting him.

In the grey dawn Siena halted on the far side of a grey flat and peered through the mists on his back trail. Something moved out among the shadows, a grey shape that crept slowly, uttering a mournful cry.

"Siena is trailed by a wolf," muttered the chief.

Yet he waited, and saw that the wolf was an Indian. He raised the fatal shooting stick.

As the Indian staggered forward, Siena recognised the robe of silver fox and marten, his gift to Emihiyah. He laughed in mockery. It was a Cree trick. Tillimanqua had led the pursuit disguised in his sister's robe. Baroma would find his son dead on the Great Slave's trail.

"Siena!" came the strange, low cry.

It was the cry that had haunted him like the voice on the wind. He leaped as a bounding deer.

Out of the grey fog burned dusky eyes half veiled by dusky hair, and little hands that he knew wavered as fluttering leaves. "Emihiyah comes," she said.

"Siena waits," he replied.

Far to the northward he led his bride and his people, far beyond the old home on the green-white, thundering Athabasca, god-forsaken river; and there, on the lonely shores of an inland sea, he fathered the Great Slave Tribe.

www.ingramcontent.com/pod-product-compliance
Lightning Source LLC
Chambersburg PA
CBHW030136260626
47156CB00008B/2972